Tiddler

By Julia Donaldson

Illustrated by Axel Scheffler

Scholastic Canada Ltd.

Toronto New York London Auckland Sydney
Mexico City New Delhi Hong Kong Buenos Aires

Once there was a fish and his name was Tiddler.

He wasn't much to look at, with his plain grey scales.

But Tiddler was a fish with a big imagination.
He blew small bubbles but he told tall tales.

"Sorry I'm late. I was riding on a seahorse."
"Sorry I'm late. I was flying with a ray."

"Sorry I'm late. I was diving with a dolphin."

Tiddler told a different story every day.

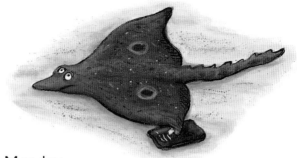

At nine o'clock on Monday,
Miss Skate called the register.
"Little Johnny Dory?"

"Yes, Miss Skate."

"Rabbitfish?" "Yes, Miss."

"Redfin?" "Yes, Miss."

"Tiddler? Tiddler?

Tiddler's late!"

"Sorry I'm late. I was swimming round a shipwreck.

I swam into a treasure chest, and someone closed the lid.

I bashed and I thrashed till a mermaid let me out again."

"Oh, no, she didn't." **"Oh, yes, she did."**

"It's only a story," said Rabbitfish and Redfin.

"Just a silly story," said Dragonfish and Dab.

"I *like* Tiddler's story,"
said Little Johnny Dory,

And he told it to his granny, who told it to a crab.

At nine o'clock on Tuesday, Miss Skate called the register.

"Little Johnny Dory?" "Yes, Miss Skate."

"Spiderfish?" "Yes, Miss." "Sunfish?" "Yes, Miss."

"Tiddler? Tiddler?

Tiddler's late!"

"Sorry I'm late, Miss. I set off really early
But on the way to school I was captured by a squid.
I wriggled and I struggled
   till a turtle came and rescued me."
"Oh, no, he didn't." **"Oh, yes, he did."**

"It's only a story," said Spiderfish and Sunfish.

"Just a silly story," said Devilfish and Dace.

 "I *love* Tiddler's story,"
said Little Johnny Dory,

And he told it to his granny,
who told it to a plaice . . .

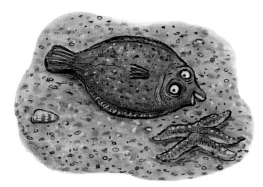

Who told it to a starfish,

who told it to a seal,

Who told it to a lobster,

who told it to an eel . . .

At nine o'clock on Wednesday, Tiddler was dawdling,
Dreaming up a story, his tallest story yet.

Lost inside his story,

he didn't see the fishing boat.

He didn't hear the fishermen. He didn't spot . . .

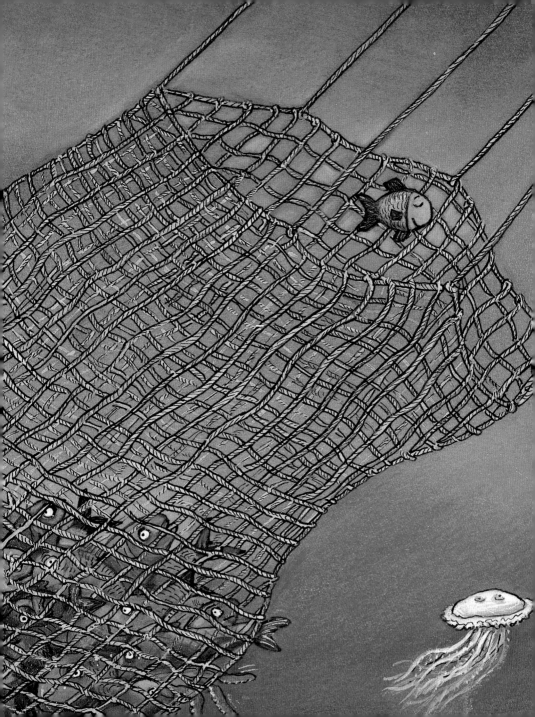

. . . the net.

Meanwhile, in the schoolroom,
Miss Skate called the register.
"Little Johnny Dory?"

"Yes, Miss Skate."

"Leopardfish?" "Yes, Miss."

"Leaf Fish?" "Yes, Miss."

"Tiddler? Tiddler?

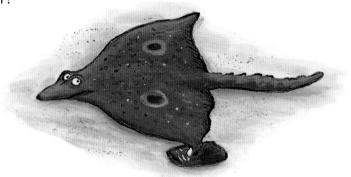

Tiddler's late!"

Ten o'clock . . .   eleven o'clock. Still no Tiddler!

Twelve o'clock, lunchtime. Where could he be?

Far away, the fishermen were hauling in their fishing net . . .

"This one's just a tiddler.
We'll throw it back to sea."

Tiddler was lost in the
middle of the ocean
Where strange lights
glimmered . . .

. . . and strange fish flew.

He swam around in circles.

He shivered in the seaweed.
But then he heard a story,
a story that he knew . . .

"Tiddler rode a seahorse. Tiddler met a mermaid.
Tiddler met a turtle, who saved him from a squid.

Tiddler found a shipwreck. Tiddler found a treasure chest."
"Oh, no, he didn't." **"Oh, yes, he did."**

Tiddler peeped out,
  and he saw a shoal of anchovies.
"Excuse me, can you tell me
  where you heard that tale?"
"We heard it from a shrimp,
  but we don't know where *she* heard it."

And they took him to the shrimp, who said,
"I heard it from a whale."

"I heard it from a herring."

"I heard it from an eel."

"I heard it from a lobster."

"I heard it from a seal."

"I heard it from a starfish."

"I heard it from a plaice."

The plaice said, "Just a minute, don't I recognize your face?"

"I'm Tiddler," said Tiddler.

"I'm tracking down my story."

The plaice replied, "I heard it from
my neighbour, Granny Dory."

One o'clock,   two o'clock . . . still no Tiddler.

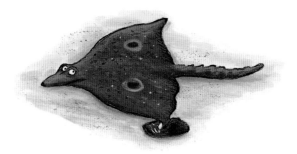

Nearly hometime. Where could he be?

Just as the fishes were finishing their lessons . . .

in swam Tiddler

at half past three!

"Sorry I'm late but I swam into a fishing net.
I managed to escape, and I swam away and hid.
I was lost, I was scared, but
   a **story** led me home again."
"Oh, no, it didn't." **"Oh, yes, it did."**

"It's just another story," said
Leopardfish and Leaf Fish.

"Just a silly story," said
Butterfish and Blue.

"It isn't just a story," said
Little Johnny Dory . . .

And he told it to a writer friend . . .

who wrote it down for you.

For Luca – A.S.
For Liam and his dad at the Bermuda Aquarium – J.D.

Scholastic Canada Ltd.
604 King Street West, Toronto, Ontario M5V 1E1, Canada

Scholastic Inc.
557 Broadway, New York, NY 10012, USA

Scholastic Australia Pty Limited
PO Box 579, Gosford, NSW 2250, Australia

Scholastic New Zealand Limited
Private Bag 94407, Botany, Manukau 2163, New Zealand

Scholastic Children's Books
Euston House, 24 Eversholt Street, London NW1 1DB, UK

www.scholastic.ca

Library and Archives Canada Cataloguing in Publication

Donaldson, Julia, author
Tiddler : the story-telling fish / by Julia Donaldson ; illustrated
by Axel Scheffler.
Previously published: United Kingdom: Scholastic, 2014.
ISBN 978-1-4431-4898-6 (paperback)
1. Readers (Primary). 2. Readers--Animals.
I. Scheffler, Axel, illustrator II. Title.
PE1119.D66 2017   428.6   C2016-904687-7

Text copyright © 2007 by Julia Donaldson.
Illustrations copyright © 2007 by Axel Scheffler.
First published in the UK by Scholastic Children's Books, 2007.
This edition published by Scholastic Canada Ltd. in 2017.

6 5 4 3 2 1   Printed in Malaysia 108   17 18 19 20 21